SADDLEBACK *Classics*

The
Count of
Monte Cristo

ALEXANDRE DUMAS

ADAPTED BY

Stephen Feinstein

SADDLEBACK
EDUCATIONAL PUBLISHING

The Count of Monte Cristo
Gulliver's Travels
The Hound of the Baskervilles
The Jungle Book
The Last of the Mohicans
Oliver Twist
The Prince and the Pauper
The Three Musketeers

Development and Production: Laurel Associates, Inc.
Cover and Interior Art: Black Eagle Productions

SADDLEBACK EDUCATIONAL PUBLISHING
Three Watson
Irvine, CA 92618-2767

Website: www.sdlback.com

ISBN 1-56254-283-4

Printed in the United States of America
11 10 09 08 07 06   9 8 7 6 5 4 3 2 1

CONTENTS

1 The Return of the *Pharaon* 5

2 Falsely Accused............................ 13

3 A Man Without Hope 18

4 The Escape 22

5 The Treasure Cave 30

6 The Priest and the Innkeeper 35

7 "An Eye for an Eye!" 41

8 Arrival in Paris.............................. 47

9 Mysterious Deaths........................ 52

10 Blinded by Greed 58

11 Web of Revenge 63

12 The Power of Love 71

§ 1 The Return of the *Pharaon*

On the 24th of February, 1815, a ship called the *Pharaon* sailed into the harbor at the French city of Marseilles. The fine three-masted sailing vessel was returning from a voyage to Italy. A lively crowd had gathered at the dock. In 1815, the arrival of such a ship was always an exciting event. But as the *Pharaon* came closer, the people in the crowd grew quiet. They began to worry that something was not right. For some reason, the ship's crew looked sad, and the men were going about their work slowly and in silence.

One man in the crowd seemed especially concerned. Monsieur Morrel, the wealthy owner of the ship, jumped into a small boat and rowed out to meet the *Pharaon*. As he drew nearer, he looked up and saw a young sailor standing by the railing. The tall young man had fine dark eyes and hair as black as coal.

"Ah, is that you, Dantes?" cried the man in the rowboat. "All of you on board are looking pretty gloomy. Tell me—what has happened?"

"A terrible thing, Monsieur Morrel," Dantes said sadly. "We have lost our brave Captain Leclere. He died of fever, and we had to bury him at sea."

"Well, this is very sad indeed," said Monsieur Morrel. "I am sorry to hear this, Monsieur Dantes. What about the cargo?"

"You may be assured that it is all safe and sound," said Dantes. He ordered the other sailors to lower the sails. Then he dropped a rope to the man in the rowboat. Monsieur Morrel grabbed the rope and climbed aboard the *Pharaon*. "Here is Monsieur Danglars, your ship's purser," Dantes said. "He can go over the accounts with you. Please excuse me now while I order the crew to drop anchor."

As Dantes walked away, Danglars frowned. "Look at him giving orders to the crew!" he said to Monsieur Morrel. "The boy is only 19 years old! He acts as if he is already captain of the ship!"

"And you think I shouldn't give him the job?" asked Monsieur Morrel. "Look! The men seem to like him. They work well under his orders."

"Captain Leclere had grown old between sky and ocean," said Danglars, a man of about 35. "You are an important man, Monsieur Morrel. A ship belonging to someone like you needs a captain who has spent many years at sea."

"But it seems to me that Edmond Dantes is doing a fine job, even though he is still a young man," said Monsieur Morrel.

"Yes," said Danglars, looking toward Dantes with hatred and envy in his eyes. He had hoped that *he* would be named captain—even though he was disliked by the crew. "Dantes is young and sure of himself. The captain was hardly dead when Dantes stepped in and took command. As the first mate, it was his duty to do so. But he made us lose a day and a half needlessly. There was no good reason for him to go ashore on the Isle of Elba."

Monsieur Morrel called out to Dantes and asked him to come over. He then took Dantes aside and asked, "Why did you stop at the Isle of Elba?"

Dantes explained that the captain, as he lay dying, had ordered him to go there. Captain Leclere had sent him to deliver a package to Marshal Bertrand, a man who was living there.

Speaking in a low voice, Monsieur Morrel asked,

"Did you see Napoleon while you were there?"

Dantes said that he had indeed seen the former emperor of France. Napoleon had been living on Elba since being driven from power. Everyone knew what he was waiting for. At the right time, he would return to France and overthrow King Louis XVIII. "He seemed to be in good health," Dantes added. "And he was pleased to hear that the ship belonged to you."

"I am glad you stopped at Elba," said Monsieur Morrel with a smile. "You did well. And now, Edmond, I would like to invite you to dine with my family tonight."

"Forgive me, Monsieur Morrel, but I cannot accept your kind invitation," said Dantes. "First I must visit my father, whom I have not seen in some time. Then my fiancée, Mercedes. And that reminds me—I shall have to ask you for two weeks leave. Mercedes and I are going to be married. After that, I must travel to Paris."

"Very well, take the time you need," said Monsieur Morrel. "But make sure you are back here in three months—for the *Pharaon* cannot sail without you. I am making you captain."

Dantes' eyes filled with joy. "Monsieur Morrel!"

he cried excitedly. "To become captain has been my dream! Don't doubt me, sir. I will certainly be back in time. You can count on me!"

After thanking Monsieur Morrel, Dantes went ashore. He quickly made his way to his father's little house. The old man had not been expecting him. With a cry of joy, he threw his arms around his handsome young son.

Dantes noticed that his father looked pale. "What is it, Father? Are you ill?" he said. "You don't look well. Haven't you been getting enough to eat?"

Looking around the house, Dantes saw that the kitchen shelves were nearly empty. "Why is there no food in the house?" he cried. "Before I left, I gave you 200 francs."

"Don't you remember that you owed 140 francs to our neighbor, Caderousse the tailor?" said the old man. "Shortly after you went away, he demanded the money. When I paid him, I had only 60 francs to last me for three months."

Dantes was furious with the tailor. But before he had a chance to say so, there was a knock at the door. It was Caderousse. He smiled at Dantes and said, "So you have come back, Edmond! I've heard your good news. You are a very lucky man."

Dantes was too angry to be pleasant. "Yes," he said coldly. Then he rudely turned away from their visitor and gave his father money to buy food. "Father," he said, "now that I have seen you, I must go see Mercedes." With that, he rushed outside and hurried to the nearby village where Mercedes lived.

When Dantes arrived at Mercedes Herrera's house, he called out her name and she ran to open the door. As soon as he stepped inside, the two fell into each other's arms. Then suddenly, Dantes saw someone else in the room. Almost hidden in the shadows, a curly-haired young man was glaring at him.

"I beg your pardon," said Dantes. "I didn't see that there were three of us." Turning to Mercedes, he said, "Who is this man?"

"I hope he will be your friend, Edmond, for he is my friend Fernand Mondego," Mercedes answered sweetly.

Dantes held out his hand to Fernand. But the scowling young man stood still as a statue and said not a word. Mercedes had failed to mention that just minutes before, Fernand had asked her to marry him. Of course, she had told Fernand that she could not—because she would love Edmond

Dantes for as long as she would live.

Mercedes insisted that Fernand shake Dantes' hand in friendship. But as the curly-haired man did so, a wave of hatred swept over him. He turned and fled the house. Running down the street, he cried out, "Oh! How can I get rid of Dantes?"

As Fernand passed by a tavern, a voice called out to him. "Hey, Fernand, where are you going? Why don't you join us for a drink?" Fernand stopped and looked around. At a small table were Caderousse and Danglars. Fernand went over and sat down with them.

As the three shared a bottle of wine, they talked about Dantes' good fortune. At only 19, he was about to become captain of the *Pharaon*. What's more, he was also about to marry the beautiful girl of his dreams! It wasn't fair, they agreed. Why should a young upstart like Dantes have all the good luck? Caderousse and Danglars were filled with envy, and Fernand was filled with hatred.

Just then, Dantes and Mercedes walked by. "Tell us, Edmond," Caderousse called out, banging on the table. "When is the wedding to take place?"

The smiling couple stopped to talk to the men. "Perhaps as soon as tomorrow or the next day. Of course, you are all invited to share in our happiness at the betrothal feast. It will be held right here in this tavern."

"Why are you in such a hurry?" Danglars asked. "After all, the *Pharaon* will not put out to sea for another three months."

"I must go to Paris to honor a promise I made to Captain Leclere," said Dantes. "But don't worry. I plan to go straight there and back again."

As Dantes and Mercedes went on their way, peaceful and happy, the three jealous men went on talking. Then Danglars remembered something. Dantes had been carrying a letter just after he had visited Marshal Bertrand on Elba!

"I'll bet he has to deliver that letter to Paris," Danglars thought to himself. "This gives me an idea! Dantes, my friend, you may not become captain of the *Pharaon* after all." Saying nothing, Danglars smiled at Fernand and Caderousse—but there was a hard, cold look in his eyes.

 # Falsely Accused

The betrothal feast of Dantes and Mercedes took place the very next day. As the guests began to gather at the tavern, Dantes said, "I can't believe how lucky I am. In fact, I worry that I may have found happiness *too* easily!"

No sooner had he spoken than there were three loud knocks on the tavern door. "Open in the name of the law!" a loud voice demanded.

A uniformed man burst into the room. "Edmond Dantes, I arrest you in the name of the law," said the police officer.

"There must be some mistake," Dantes gasped. But before Edmond or any of the guests could say another word, the officer led him away.

As he was dragged to a carriage outside the tavern, Dantes assured Mercedes that he would return as soon as the mistake was cleared up.

Monsieur Morrel followed Dantes to Marseilles

in his own carriage. When he returned to the tavern several hours later, he brought bad news.

"It is a far more serious matter than we had thought," he said. "*I*, of course, believe that Dantes is innocent. But he has been accused of being a secret agent for Napoleon!"

"I had my suspicions when he stopped at the Isle of Elba," Danglars said. "But I didn't say anything to anyone."

"I trust that Dantes will be able to clear his name," Monsieur Morrel said confidently. "But in the meantime the *Pharaon* is without a captain. So until Dantes is released, I appoint you, Mr. Danglars, to take command of my ship."

Danglars nodded modestly, but to himself he thought, "So far, my plan is working perfectly!"

The guests began to leave the tavern. Dantes' friends took charge of his brokenhearted father. Fernand looked after Mercedes, who seemed to be numb with disappointment.

That same day another betrothal was being celebrated. In the wealthier part of Marseilles, an ambitious young lawyer named Gerard de Villefort announced that he was going to marry Renee, the daughter of the Marquis and Marquise of Saint-Meran. Villefort was the official prosecutor of Marseilles. But he had hopes of rising to a much higher political office. Marrying Renee was part of his plan. Her powerful family had close connections to the court of King Louis XVIII.

The guests at this party were all royalists. As they lifted their glasses to their monarch, the Marquise said, "I wonder what Napoleon's followers see in that man."

Villefort sneered. "Napoleon has told them that all men are equal," he said.

"I'm a bit surprised you don't agree with him,"

said the Marquise. "After all, your own father is a follower of Napoleon, is he not?"

Villefort's face turned red. "I am not *at all* like Noirtier, my father. I've even taken a different name! Everyone knows that I am loyal to the king!"

Just then, a servant entered and handed Villefort a note. "It seems that a plot by Napoleon's supporters has been discovered," he said, after reading the note. "This note is not signed. But whoever wrote it accuses Edmond Dantes of carrying a letter from Napoleon. The police are holding Dantes until I arrive. I must leave now and question him tonight."

The police were waiting for Villefort at the law courts. Monsieur Morrel, who was also there, quickly told him that a mistake had been made. Dantes was an innocent man. "We shall see about that," said Villefort.

After Dantes had answered all of Villefort's questions, it was clear that the young man was indeed innocent. He seemed to know nothing about Napoleon's followers.

"I'm sorry for your trouble," said Villefort. "Whoever wrote that note is clearly a liar. Give me the letter, and go now." He smiled at Dantes.

Dantes was overjoyed. He gladly handed the letter to Villefort. Before looking at it, however, Villefort said, "By the way—to whom were you supposed to deliver this letter?"

"To a Monsieur Noirtier, in Paris," said Dantes.

The smile froze on Villefort's face. "Nobody must learn that my father was to receive a letter from Napoleon!" he thought to himself. "My future would be destroyed!"

"On second thought, this letter *could* cause problems," Villefort said in a cool voice. "You'll have to stay here tonight. And I'll destroy the letter. It is evidence that can be used against you."

"Thank you, monsieur," said Dantes.

An hour or so after dark, four policemen came for Dantes and led him outside. But instead of setting him free, they took him to the harbor and put him in a small boat.

"Where are you taking me?" Dantes cried out.

One of the policemen pointed to a steep black rock that rose from the sea in the distance. Dantes' heart sank! It was the Chateau d'If—the terrible prison from which no man ever escapes!

3 A Man Without Hope

During his first few days in the jail cell, Dantes raged at the prison guards. *"I'm an innocent man!"* he shouted. "A terrible mistake has been made!" When the guards ignored him, he grew even angrier. They brought him some bread, but Dantes ate nothing. Finally, however, Dantes grew calm. If there was to be any hope for him, he must get word to those who cared about him.

The next day, Dantes told a guard that he wished to write a letter to Mercedes. He promised to pay the man if the letter was delivered. The guard laughed loudly. "I'd be a fool to help you! I could lose my job if they find out I helped a follower of Napoleon." Now Dantes saw that he was completely cut off from the outside world. He demanded to speak to the prison warden.

"That's not possible," the guard said coldly. Dantes saw red. He erupted in fury, picking up a wooden stool and swinging it over his head. The guard said, "That's enough! I'll go tell the warden." Soon he returned with three other guards. "This fellow has gone mad," they all agreed. "We must move him to the dungeon."

The dungeon was deep down in the lower part of the Chateau d'If. There Dantes remained alone with his thoughts. The days turned into months, the months into years. At first Dantes was angry much of the time. Then his anger faded, and he sank into a deep sadness. From time to time he thought about Mercedes and the happiness they might have shared. Tears would come to his eyes. For long periods he went without eating. But he always kept hoping that somehow, some way, he would be set free. He knew that he was an innocent man, so he prayed to God for justice. In spite of his prayers, however, he was still a prisoner.

Six years passed, then eight, then ten. All the while Dantes remained in prison, he knew nothing of what had happened on the outside. Soon after Dantes' arrest, Villefort had gone to see King Louis. He had told the king that Napoleon was plotting to return to France. The king had rewarded Villefort by awarding him the cross of the Legion of Honor.

Soon after this, Napoleon had escaped from Elba and returned to France. As he and his followers marched toward Paris, people rushed to join his army. King Louis fled the country, and Napoleon returned triumphantly. He then set up his Court of the Hundred Days to reign as emperor of France a second time.

Villefort was allowed to keep his job as prosecutor, because Noirtier, his father, was a friend of Napoleon. Twice during this time, Monsieur Morrel had pleaded with Villefort to release Dantes from prison. But each time Villefort had refused to act.

Although Napoleon had many supporters in France, he also had many enemies. Shortly after his return, supporters of King Louis banded together and rose up against him. Fighting broke out. Then Napoleon's forces were attacked by the German and British armies. Napoleon's final defeat came at the Battle of Waterloo. There he was taken prisoner by the British, and King Louis was returned to his throne. Napoleon was exiled for life to the island of St. Helena, a dot of land far out in the South Atlantic.

Dantes knew nothing of these events. Nor had

he heard anything about the important people in his life. Mercedes had been filled with grief after Dantes' arrest. Fernand had spent time with her every day. He was very kind to her, but for a long time Mercedes was blind to all but Dantes. She didn't know where Dantes was being held or even if he was still alive.

Five months after Dantes' arrest, King Louis was once again in power. By this time Dantes' father had lost all hope for his son. He became ill and died in Mercedes' arms. As a loyal friend, Monsieur Morrel paid for the funeral. This generous act was also an act of bravery. Monsieur Morrel could have been imprisoned himself for helping the family of a man accused of supporting Napoleon.

As the years went by, Dantes slowly began to lose all hope of ever being free again. The strong young man ate less and less and became weaker and weaker. At last he no longer cared whether he lived or died.

4 The Escape

One night, while lying curled up against a wall, Dantes was startled by a dull sound. This steady, scraping noise was different from the usual sounds made by the rats. It was the sound of a tool being worked against stone!

"Could this be the sound of a prisoner trying to dig his way out?" Dantes wondered. With a shiver of hope, he picked up a stone and knocked several times on the wall. The scraping sound stopped. But the next night the sound started again.

Dantes began to use the iron handle from his food pot as a tool. He dug at the plaster between the stones in the wall. In three days of hard work he had loosened a large stone. Dantes pushed his bed against the wall so the guard wouldn't see what he was up to.

For the next few days Dantes dug deeper into the wall. Then one day his iron tool suddenly slid off a smooth surface. A wooden beam blocked his way! "Oh, my God!" he prayed. "Have pity on me! Don't let me die with nothing to hope for!"

"Who speaks of God and of hopelessness at the same time? Who are you?" a soft voice whispered.

"Edmond Dantes, a sailor," Dantes declared.

"Tell me—what's on the other side of your cell?" asked the voice.

"The passage that leads to the courtyard," Dantes answered.

"Oh, no!" the voice gasped. "I've made a terrible mistake! I thought I was digging a hole in the *outer* wall. I was hoping to jump into the sea. If I could swim away, I thought I might be saved."

"Tell me who you are," said Dantes.

"I am—I am prisoner number 27," said the voice.

"Don't you trust me?" said Dantes. "I swear that I won't betray you! We will escape together. If we cannot escape, we can at least talk together."

"Hide your work. I will come to you tomorrow," said the voice.

For the first time in many years, Dantes felt a glimmer of happiness. He was not going to be alone anymore! With any luck, he might even gain his freedom. All day long, he walked up and down in his cell, his heart beating wildly.

The next morning, after the first shift of guards had left, Dantes heard the sound of falling stones. The other prisoner climbed through the hole and into Dantes' cell! Dantes threw his arms around the white-haired old man.

The old man introduced himself as Father Faria. He quickly warmed up to Dantes. After being isolated for such a long time, the two lonely men felt great joy in each other's company. Soon they were telling each other their stories.

Father Faria was a learned man of the church. To help pass the time in prison, he had written a book. He had made a pen out of fish bones and used strips of cloth from his shirts as paper. He had also made a knife out of an old iron candlestick. "Come with me to my cell," he said to Dantes. "I'll show it to you."

The two crawled through the secret tunnel in the wall to the old priest's cell. There Dantes told his own story. Father Faria listened carefully and asked many questions. Finally, he pointed out how both Danglars and Fernand had something to gain from Dantes' arrest. Then, he asked, "To whom were you supposed to deliver that letter?"

"A Monsieur Noirtier," said Dantes.

"I knew a fellow named Noirtier. He was a follower of Napoleon. And tell me again—what was the prosecutor's name?" asked the priest.

"Villefort," said Dantes.

The priest laughed. "I might have known!" he said, shaking his head. "Oh, you poor man! That prosecutor is Noirtier's son! No wonder he sent you to the Chateau d'If."

Dantes remembered how Villefort had gone pale at the mention of Noirtier's name. His mind was racing. Suddenly it was all becoming clear to him. "I must be alone to think this over!" Dantes cried. He rushed back to his own cell. There he fell on his bed. For many hours he didn't move. A violent storm of thoughts crashed around in his head. By the time he got up, he had made a terrible plan of revenge.

The next day the old priest said he was sorry that he had helped Dantes understand what had happened to him. When Dantes asked why, Father Faria said sadly, "Because I see in your heart a darkness that was not there before."

"Let us speak of something else," said Dantes. "I have very little education and you are a man of great learning. Will you teach me?"

Within a year, Dantes had indeed learned a great deal about history, science, and math, as well as several languages. Then one day, the old priest told Dantes about his new plan.

They would escape by climbing through the window in the passage outside their cells. First they would dig a new tunnel below the passage. Then they would loosen the stones in a section of the passage floor so the night guard would fall through. Finally, Dantes and Father Faria would tie up the guard and climb through the window.

Fifteen months later, they were almost ready. They had dug the tunnel and loosened the stones in the passage. But as they were working one day, the priest suddenly cried out and fell down.

"What's the matter?" cried Dantes.

Father Faria's face was pale. "I have a terrible sickness and I feel an attack coming," he said. "Help me! I must get back to my cell at once. I have some medicine there."

Dantes helped the old priest back to his cell. "I need ten drops of the red liquid in that little bottle," Father Faria gasped. "Give it to me even if I seem to be dead!" At that, he began to shake as his face turned very pale. Then he lay still.

Dantes administered the medicine. After a while, the color came back to the old priest's face. He said sadly, "You will have to escape alone. I cannot move my right arm. I fear I will never be able to move it again. The next attack will kill me."

"No! We can still escape together," Dantes insisted. "I'll swim with you on my back!"

"No," said the old man. "You wouldn't get far. It's too late. I will never leave this prison now."

"In that case, I won't escape now. I'll remain here until one of us dies," said Dantes.

Father Faria was amazed at the young man's loyalty. "So be it," he said with a smile. "Come here tomorrow. I have something important to tell you."

The next morning, Father Faria showed Dantes a piece of paper. "This is my treasure, which now belongs to you!" he said. Then he explained that the paper held the secret to a great treasure hidden in a little cave on the Isle of Monte Cristo. "Many years ago I worked for Count Spada. When he died, there were no remaining members of the Spada family. So he left his papers to me—and this was among them. But I was arrested before I could find the treasure. So now it belongs to you."

"But the treasure belongs to *you*, my friend," Dantes insisted. "I have no right to it. I am not even related to you."

"Ah, but you are. You are my true son, Dantes," said the old man, "the child of my years in prison."

Dantes threw his arms around the old man and burst into tears.

A few days later, Father Faria died. Dantes saw that the old man had wrapped his own body in a cloth sack before dying.

Then an idea suddenly came to Dantes. "Since only the dead may leave here, I will take the place of the dead!" He brought Father Faria's body back to his cell and placed it under the covers on his bed. Then he returned to the priest's cell, picked up the old man's knife, and climbed into the sack. No sooner had he sewn it closed than the guards came and carried the sack outside.

"He is very heavy for such a thin old man," one of the guards grumbled. Soon Dantes heard the noise of waves breaking against rocks. Then the guards swung him into the air, and Dantes was plunging into the ocean.

$\oint$ 5 The Treasure Cave

Hungry for air, Dantes used the priest's knife to rip open the sack. He kicked his legs strongly and quickly rose to the surface. For a few seconds, he breathed deeply, but then dived again to avoid being seen. When he rose a second time, he was already 50 yards from the prison. With all his strength he plowed ahead through the waves.

A storm hit after Dantes had been swimming for an hour. It was too dark to see anything. Suddenly, his knee hit something hard. Then his hand struck something. Dantes had reached land! Weak with exhaustion, he climbed out of the sea onto a rocky shore. It was the Isle of Tiboulen.

Dantes lay down on the shore and fell asleep. An hour later, he was awakened by a loud clap of thunder. In a flash of lightning, Dantes saw a fishing boat crash against the rocks. Hearing the fishermen cry out, he rushed across the rocks to try to help them. But when he got there, the fishermen had disappeared without a trace.

The next morning, the weather had cleared. In the distance, Dantes saw an Italian ship. He thought about signaling, but then he stopped. "They might suspect that I'm an escaped prisoner," Dantes thought. Then he saw a fisherman's cap that had washed ashore. He grabbed the cap and put it on his head. "Now I have a story," he thought. "I'll tell them I'm a fisherman." With that, he dived into the sea and swam toward the ship.

Two sailors pulled Dantes out of the water. "Bless you! You have saved my life," Dantes cried. "Our fishing boat crashed against the rocks in the storm. I'm the only survivor."

"What are we going to do with you?" asked the bad-tempered captain.

"I'm a good sailor, sir. I can be of use to you."

"Very well," said the captain. "We can always use an extra hand." He told one of the sailors to bring some food and drink for Dantes.

After a while, Dantes said, "By the way, what year is this? I still can't think clearly—my head took a very hard knock in that storm."

When a sailor told him it was 1829, Dantes

shook his head in wonder. He had lost track of time in the Chateau d'If. It was hard to believe he had been a prisoner for 14 years! That meant he was now 33 years old! He thought about Mercedes, and wondered where she was.

Dantes soon discovered that the captain and his crew were smugglers. They sailed around the Mediterranean, trading stolen goods. Once the ship passed close to the Isle of Monte Cristo. But Dantes had no chance to go ashore.

One day, the captain said that he had arranged a meeting with another crew of smugglers—at the Isle of Monte Cristo! This was the news that Dantes had been waiting for. He tried not to show his excitement as they got closer to the island.

Nothing lived on the lonely island except wild goats. While the two crews did their trading, Dantes excused himself to go out hunting. He killed a goat and brought it back for the crew. While they cooked it, Dantes continued to explore the island.

On his way back, the sailors saw Dantes slip and fall on the rocks. When they reached him, he was lying on the ground. He said he had a sharp pain in his knee, and a terrible ache in his back.

"Carry him back to the ship," said the captain.

"No," said Dantes. "I cannot be moved now—I'm in too much pain. Leave me here. I should be fine after a few days of rest. I'll be back on my feet when you return for me."

"But you will die of hunger," the captain objected. "We cannot leave you like this."

"Just leave me some food, a gun, and an ax," said Dantes. None of their pleas could shake his wish to remain on the island alone. Finally, the crew brought Dantes the items he had asked for.

In less than an hour, the ship had disappeared from view. Dantes got up and jumped about on the rocks like a wild goat. At last he could look for the treasure! The island was small. It didn't take Dantes long to find the cave. He no longer had the old priest's paper, but the secret was in his head.

The words on Father Faria's paper had said, "in the farthest corner of the second cave." Dantes soon found a crack in the wall of the first cave. He began digging there, using his ax. At last the stones gave way, and Dantes climbed into the second cave.

He went to the farthest corner and began looking around. Soon he found it—a great wooden chest with iron bands! Dantes' heart was pounding. He put the sharp end of the ax under the lid and

opened the chest. He could not believe his eyes! The chest was indeed filled with treasure. Dantes saw piles of bright gold coins, gold ingots, and jewels. He scooped up handfuls of diamonds, pearls, and rubies and let them fall through his fingers. He wondered if he was dreaming.

In his excitement, Dantes rushed outside the cave. He ran about on the rocks, shouting like a madman. Then he went back inside the cave. Sure enough, the treasure was still there. It was real, and it was his! Dantes fell on his knees, saying a prayer that God alone could understand.

6 The Priest and the Innkeeper

While Dantes was still in prison, Caderousse had become the owner of a small country inn in the south of France. One day as he stood by the door of his inn, he saw a man on a horse in the distance. As the rider got closer, Caderousse could see that the man was a priest. He was dressed in a black robe and wore a hat with three corners.

The rider stopped in front of the inn. "Are you not Monsieur Caderousse?" he asked politely.

"Yes, monsieur. That is my name," said the innkeeper. "Can I offer you something to eat or drink?" He would never have guessed that the "priest" in front of him was none other than his old neighbor, Edmond Dantes!

"Give me a bottle of wine. Then we can talk. Are we alone?" asked the priest.

"Yes," said Caderousse. "We are alone, except for my wife. But she is sick and usually keeps to herself. Come, let's go inside."

When the priest was seated, he said, "Did you once know a sailor named Dantes?"

"I should say so! Poor Edmond. He was one of my best friends!" said Caderousse. "Do you know him? Tell me what has become of him! Is he still living? Is he free? Is he happy?"

"I'm afraid that he died a prisoner—sad and without hope," said the priest.

Caderousse's face grew pale. He wiped a tear from his eye. "Poor fellow," he said.

"You seem to have been very fond of this boy," said the priest.

"I was indeed. But I must admit that at one time I was filled with envy at his happiness," Caderousse said sadly. "Please tell me what happened to him."

The dark-eyed priest was looking very closely at Caderousse's face. "I was called to Dantes' bedside while he was dying," he said. "He said he never knew why he was in prison. He wished me to clear up the mystery. He told me that he had three good friends and a fiancée. One was named Caderousse, another Danglars, and the third Fernand. I believe the fiancée was named Mercedes.

"Anyway, before he died, Dantes gave me a

diamond that had been given to him by another prisoner." The priest took out the diamond, and Caderousse's eyes grew wide.

"Dantes said he wanted to share the diamond with those who had once loved him. He asked me to sell the diamond and divide the money into five parts," the priest explained.

"Why *five* parts?" asked Caderousse. "You only named four persons."

"The fifth share was for Dantes' father. But in Marseilles, I heard that he is dead," said the priest.

"Yes, it is only too true," said Caderousse. "The poor man died of sadness, waiting for his son who never returned. Monsieur Morrel and Mercedes brought a doctor—but it was too late."

"A sad, sad tragedy," said the priest, covering his eyes with his hand, trying to hide his tears.

"All the more sad," said Caderousse, "because Dantes' troubles were none of God's doing, but the work of two evil men!"

"Who are these two men?" asked the priest. "Tell me everything."

"The two men I speak of were very jealous of Dantes," said Caderousse. "Their names are Danglars and Fernand—Dantes' so-called *friends*!

They are the ones who accused poor Edmond of working for Napoleon. Danglars wrote an incriminating note the day before Edmond's betrothal feast, and Fernand mailed it."

"And you knew all about it—yet you did nothing to stop it?" the priest asked.

"I *wanted* to speak out, but Danglars said I would get in trouble. I was a coward, but not a criminal," Caderousse said defensively.

"I see—you just let things take their course," said the priest.

"Yes, monsieur," said Caderousse. "And I regret it night and day. I can only beg God's forgiveness."

"And who is this Monsieur Morrel you spoke of?" asked the priest. "What part did this man play in this shameful affair?"

"He is the owner of the *Pharaon*. For many months he tried to get Dantes out of prison. He also did what he could for Dantes' father," said Caderousse. "He was once a powerful man, but Monsieur Morrel has fallen on hard times since then. Several of his ships were lost at sea, and he cannot pay his debts.

"Meanwhile," Caderousse went on, "Fernand and Danglars are happy and rich. Danglars made a lot of money during the Spanish war. Then he married a rich widow. He now owns a house in Paris, and is known as *Baron* Danglars! Fernand has become a count. He fought in Greece for Ali Pasha against the Turks. When Ali Pasha died, he left a great fortune to Fernand."

"And what about Mercedes?" asked the priest. "I heard she has disappeared."

"Disappeared?" said Caderousse. "Oh, no! She is now one of the richest ladies in Paris. When Fernand came back from Greece, he told Mercedes he loved her. They were married, and had a son, Albert. So you see how unfair the world is," said Caderousse. "Everything those two fellows touched turned to gold. And everything *I've* done has failed miserably."

"You are mistaken, my friend," said the priest. "Sooner or later, God remembers us." He gave the diamond to Caderousse. "Take this; it is yours," he said. "It seems that Dantes had but one true friend." The priest said goodbye to the amazed and delighted Caderousse and rode off.

When he got back to Marseilles, Dantes found out what he needed to know about Monsieur Morrel's debts. Then several weeks later, Monsieur

Morrel received even more bad news. His last and best ship, the *Pharaon*, had gone down in a storm! Monsieur Morrel was so upset he could hardly speak.

"Is there really no money at all left?" asked his son Maximilian.

"I'm afraid we are ruined," said Monsieur Morrel as he choked back tears.

Suddenly, his daughter Julie ran into the room. "Father!" she cried. "You are saved! You are *saved*!"

"What do you mean, my child?" Monsieur Morrel asked in confusion.

Julie showed her father a bill for 287,500 francs, marked *paid*. "Where did you get this?" asked Monsieur Morrel in amazement.

"A stranger came to the door and handed it to me," said Julie. "I had never seen him before. He was gone before I could say anything."

Later that day, a small boat sailed away from Marseilles. Dantes was on board. As he looked back at the city, he thought about Monsieur Morrel. "Be happy, noble heart. May God bless you for all the good you have done. And for now, goodbye to kindness. I have rewarded the good. Now it is time to punish the wicked!"

7   "An Eye for an Eye!"

Early in the year 1831, two rich young men from Paris arrived in Rome for the Carnival. They had come to have a good time. But Albert de Morcerf, the son of Mercedes and Fernand, and his friend Franz d'Epinay, were not happy. The hotelkeeper had just told them that there were no carriages to rent in all of Rome.

"Do you expect us to *walk* around town—just like the poorest people of Rome?" Albert said to the hotelkeeper. "If there are no carriages, then find us a wagon and a pair of oxen."

Soon the hotelkeeper returned. He told the young men that they were in luck. The Count of Monte Cristo, who was also staying at the hotel, had offered to share his carriage with them.

Albert and Franz looked at each other. "Who is this count? What kind of man is he?" Franz asked the hotelkeeper.

"I don't know much about him. I'm not even sure where he comes from—perhaps Sicily, or Malta," said the hotelkeeper. "But I do know that he is very, very rich."

The next day Albert and Franz visited the count in the hotel. A servant showed them in. The suite was filled with expensive works of art, and there were costly rugs on the floor. The Count of Monte Cristo—who, of course, was none other than Edmond Dantes—greeted the young men. "Good morning, gentlemen," he said with a smile. "I am at your service."

After Albert and Franz thanked him for his kindness, the count invited them to come with him to an execution. "Two men will be put to death," said Dantes. "One of them is a young bandit who belongs to Luigi Vampa's gang. But I've had word that he will be pardoned. The other is a murderer, who will have his head cut off. I say he's getting off too easy!"

"What do you mean?" said Franz. "It doesn't sound to me like an easy way to die."

"Think about it," said Dantes. "What if a man had killed members of *your* family and caused you to suffer for many years? Do you think that just a few moments of pain would be enough of a punishment? I don't think so."

"Then how do you think he should pay for his crime?" Franz asked.

"If *I* had been made to suffer for a long time," Dantes cried, "I would want to be sure that he did, too!" A look of hatred came over his face, and his voice rose. "Oh, yes, I believe in an eye for an eye, and a tooth for a tooth!"

The count's furious outburst made Franz uncomfortable. "I believe that revenge can turn against you," he said nervously.

"Perhaps if you are poor and foolish," said Dantes, "but surely not if you are rich and smart. Let us go now to the execution."

Sure enough, the young bandit was set free. As the other young man was executed, Albert and Franz closed their eyes. Dantes, however, watched very carefully. "My enemies will not get off this easily," he thought. "My revenge will be slow. Yes, they will suffer for a long time."

Soon it was time for the Carnival. Dantes and his two young guests put on their costumes and masks. As they rode through the streets in Dantes' carriage, they passed a carriage full of women.

Albert threw flowers. One of the women caught the blossoms. Then she lifted her mask and gave Albert a smile. He could see that she was quite beautiful.

The next day, Albert received a note from the woman, suggesting that they meet. That night, Franz and Albert walked down the street. The streets were lit by thousands of Carnival candles. When they saw the woman, Franz stayed back and Albert went to her. Franz saw them walk off arm in arm. Soon a loud bell rang. The Carnival was over for the night. The candles were blown out, and the streets went dark.

When Albert failed to return to the hotel the next morning, Franz began to worry. Then he received a note from the bandit Luigi Vampa. It said that Albert would die unless Franz paid a ransom of 4,000 piasters! Franz did not have that much money with him. The only thing he could think of was to ask the Count of Monte Cristo for help.

Dantes asked Franz who had brought the note. Franz said the man was waiting downstairs in the street, so Dantes called to him from the window. When the man came up to the room, Dantes said, "Why, you're the young bandit who was set free!"

The man fell to his knees and kissed Dantes'

hand. "I'm glad you found out who saved your life," Dantes said. "Since you are one of Luigi Vampa's men, he owes me a favor now. So now you must tell me what happened to Albert. Where is Luigi Vampa holding him?"

The young bandit explained everything. He said that the woman Albert had met was Luigi Vampa's girlfriend. No other man was allowed to come anywhere near her. That's why Albert was being held prisoner in the dark and dangerous catacombs beneath the city. "I can take you to him," said the young bandit.

"It's a good thing you came to me," Dantes said to Franz. "You might never have seen your friend alive again." With that, both men set out for the catacombs. The young bandit led them through several dark passages. Finally they came to a large room lit by a small lamp. Sitting in a circle of lamplight was Luigi Vampa. Some rough-looking men who were standing guard pointed their guns at Dantes.

"My dear Vampa," said Dantes, "is this any way to repay me for saving your friend?"

Vampa ordered his men to put down their guns. When Dantes explained that Albert was his friend,

Vampa set him free. Later, Albert tried to thank Dantes for saving him. "I owe you my life. How can I ever repay you?"

Dantes smiled. "You do not really owe me so much. But come to think of it, I plan to visit Paris soon. I have never been to that great city before, and I don't know anyone there. I wonder if you would be so kind as to introduce me to people."

"I would be delighted to!" Albert cried out happily. Then, after agreeing to meet the count sometime later in Paris, Albert and Franz said goodbye and left.

Dantes thought about the events of the past week. Everything that had happened to the two young men had been part of Dantes' plan of revenge. He had arranged all the details. Nothing had been left to chance. But of course the two young men had no idea of this.

Later that day, Franz said to Albert, "I have a bad feeling about the Count of Monte Cristo!"

"What!" said Albert. "How can you say such a thing? He has been so kind to us."

"I'm not sure—but there's something *strange* about him. Perhaps it's my imagination, but he makes me worry," said Franz with a shrug.

Arrival in Paris

Three months later, Albert invited a group of his friends to breakfast at his home in Paris. Among the guests was Maximilian Morrel, the son of the ship owner. Albert's friends had been told to expect an important guest of honor—the Count of Monte Cristo. But none had ever heard of him.

Then Dantes walked into the room, dressed in the latest Parisian style. Albert said to the guests, "Gentlemen, this is the Count of Monte Cristo—the wonderful man who saved me from the clutches of the bandit Luigi Vampa."

Dantes' thoughts were focused on the revenge he was planning. But nobody could have guessed such a thing. The Count of Monte Cristo seemed very friendly. Over breakfast, Dantes charmed the guests with colorful tales of his adventures.

It was not surprising that Albert's home would be the first place Dantes visited in Paris. After all, it was also the home of Mercedes and Fernand, Albert's parents. Fernand was now called the *Count* de Morcerf—a title he had purchased.

After the guests had left, Albert led Dantes into the salon to meet his parents. Although Fernand was much older now, Dantes recognized his old enemy at once. But Fernand had not a clue as to Dantes' true identity. "It is an honor to meet a great soldier such as yourself," said Dantes.

Fernand smiled and shook Dantes' hand. Just then, Mercedes entered the room. "Ah, here is my mother," said Albert. When Mercedes saw Dantes, her face turned white. She leaned against the wall.

"What's the matter?" Fernand asked. "Is the heat in this room too much for you, my dear?"

Albert rushed to his mother's side. "Are you ill, Mother?" he asked worriedly.

"I'm fine, Albert," said Mercedes. Then she turned to Dantes and said, "It upsets me to think what might have happened to my son had you not saved him. Monsieur, I bless you and thank you from the bottom of my heart."

Dantes bowed low. "It was but a simple deed," he said. "Any man would have done as much."

"Dear sir, would you do us the honor of

spending the day with us?" Mercedes asked.

Dantes said that nothing would please him more. But, he explained, he had business to attend to. With that, he bowed once more and took his leave.

When Dantes arrived at his new home in Paris, Haydee was waiting there for him. She was a beautiful young Greek woman. When she was only a child, Dantes had rescued her from slavery in Turkey. He had taken care of the poor orphan ever since. "You are so beautiful, sweet Haydee," Dantes said to her. "When the young men of Paris see you, they will all want to meet you."

"But I only want to be with *you*," Haydee cried. "I love only you!"

"No, Haydee," Dantes laughed. "I'm old enough to be your father! Your love for me is like a daughter's love for her father."

"I remember my father," the young woman said. "My love for you is different."

A few days later, Dantes carried out the next step in his plan. He told his servant to watch out for a carriage pulled by two runaway horses. Following Dantes' orders, the servant ran out a few minutes later and stopped just such a carriage.

Inside the carriage were a woman and a young

boy. Dantes led them into his house. "Come inside and rest. You have nothing more to fear," said Dantes. "You are safe now!"

"But look at my poor son," cried the woman. "Edward, my child! Answer your mother! Oh, monsieur, please send for a doctor!"

"He is not hurt, madame. He has only fainted," said Dantes. Taking a small bottle from his pocket, he put a drop of red liquid on the boy's lips. Soon the boy opened his eyes.

The mother was relieved. When Dantes introduced himself, she said, "I've heard so much about you. I am Heloise de Villefort."

Of course, Dantes already knew who she was. She was Heloise, the second wife of Gerard de Villefort—the man who had sent Dantes to the Chateau d'If. When Edward reached out for the bottle of red liquid, Dantes said, "That liquid can be poisonous, if you're not careful!" Heloise was looking at the bottle with great interest. As she was leaving, she asked Dantes if he could send her some. He promised to do so.

Later that day, Dantes received a visit from Villefort. He had come to thank Dantes for saving his wife and son. "I am honored by your visit," said

Dantes in a cold voice. "I know that social status means a lot to you. You only visit important people. But I was given my position not by men, but by God. I am on a mission to reward and to punish. Only death can keep me from my mission."

Villefort wasn't sure what to make of these strange, harsh words. He said, "I believe you. You must be a truly powerful person. When you get to know me better, you will see that I am not an ordinary man, either."

Later that day, Valentine, the lovely daughter of Villefort and his first wife Renee, met with Maximilian Morrel. They were in the garden of the Villefort house. She told Maximilian that in three months she was to marry Franz d'Epinay. Her father had made the plans for her. "This makes me sad," she said. "*You* are the one I will always love."

"But I thought your stepmother didn't like Franz," said Maximilian.

"Heloise does not want me to marry anyone," said Valentine. "She knows that I will inherit all of my family's money when I marry. Then her son Edward will get nothing." At that moment, Valentine heard her grandfather calling. As she got up, Maximilian kissed her hand.

9 Mysterious Deaths

A few days later, Dantes received a visit from Danglars, who was now a rich banker known as Baron Danglars. Danglars had gotten a letter inviting him to visit the Count of Monte Cristo. Again, Dantes remained calm when he saw his old enemy. Danglars had no idea who the count really was. Many years had gone by since he had given a thought to Dantes or the *Pharaon*.

In a friendly voice, Dantes explained that he might have to borrow millions of francs. In fact, he wanted Danglars' bank to grant him unlimited credit. Danglars liked what he heard about the count, and he quickly agreed to Dantes' request.

The next day, Dantes received another guest— the illegitimate son of Villefort. Young Benedetto had been abandoned by his father at an early age. As the neglected boy had grown older, he had become a criminal. Dantes had sent for the young man as soon as he had learned of his existence.

"How would you like to become a rich young man, wear the finest clothes, and be invited to the best salons?" Dantes asked Benedetto.

The young man could hardly believe his ears. It seemed too good to be true! "If you agree," Dantes went on, "from now on your name will be Andrea Cavalcanti. You will have all the money you need. And I will teach you everything you must know to take your place in high society."

The bright young man learned quickly, and before long Dantes was satisfied with his education. Then, late one night, as the boy was getting into his carriage, he felt a hand on his shoulder. Turning around, he saw a familiar face. "*Caderousse!*" he cried. "What do you want?"

"Benedetto, my friend, it's so good to see you," said Caderousse. "I could use a ride." He climbed into the carriage after the young man. "It looks as if you've had some good luck."

Benedetto was not pleased to see Caderousse, the man who had shared his prison cell. "Listen, I have a new life now. I cannot do anything for you."

"Aren't you being a little greedy—hoarding all your good fortune for yourself?" asked Caderousse.

"Look who's talking!" said Benedetto. "*You're* the greedy one. What about that diamond the priest gave you?" He had learned that Caderousse had sold the diamond—before killing the diamond trader and keeping the diamond *and* the money.

"Ah, Benedetto," said Caderousse, "I need some money. If you don't help me, I'm afraid I'll have to tell the Count of Monte Cristo about your own crimes." Benedetto didn't know what else to do. He agreed to pay Caderousse 200 francs a month to keep him quiet.

Before long, Benedetto became known in Paris as Andrea Cavalcanti. He was welcomed into the best homes and salons. At about this time, Baron Danglars lost a lot of money when one of his businesses failed. Soon after, it was announced that his daughter, Eugenie, would marry Andrea Cavalcanti. The count had told Danglars that Cavalcanti was very rich.

Meanwhile, bad things were about to happen in the Villefort house. One morning, the Marquise, Valentine's grandmother, walked into Villefort's study. She was crying. She told Villefort that her husband had suddenly died at dawn. "I'm old and afraid," she said. "Valentine and Franz must get married right away. I want to make sure all my money goes to my dear granddaughter."

The Marquise was put to bed. A comforting drink was brought to her and placed on a small table by the bed. She reached for it and drank the whole thing. In an hour, she, too, was dead.

The doctor took Villefort aside. "I'm sorry to tell you this," said the doctor, "but the Marquise was poisoned. Tell me—is there anyone who might gain something from her death?"

Villefort couldn't believe what he was hearing. "No!" he said. "Valentine will get all of her money."

The doctor warned Villefort to keep his eyes and ears open. "If you find the guilty person, I'm sure you will do the right thing," the doctor said nervously. "You're a prosecutor, after all."

A week later, Franz came to the Villefort house to make wedding arrangements. Valentine's grandfather, Monsieur Noirtier, was brought out in his wheelchair. He had suffered a stroke, and it was difficult for him to speak. But there was something he was determined to do. At his signal, the old man's servant handed over some papers to Franz.

Franz saw that the papers were dated February 5, 1815—the date of his father's death! As Franz went on reading, his hands began to shake. The papers told about a duel that had been fought between Franz's father, General d'Epinay, and a follower of Napoleon—Monsieur Noirtier!

Franz threw down the papers. "So it was *you!*" he cried, glaring at Monsieur Noirtier. "I cannot marry the granddaughter of the man who killed my own father!" He turned and ran out of the house.

When Maximilian learned of this turn of events, he was filled with joy. He rushed to Valentine, who was also delighted. They sat down with Monsieur Noirtier to discuss plans for their marriage. It was a hot day, and Noirtier was drinking lemonade. Valentine kindly offered a glass of lemonade to Noirtier's old servant.

Then suddenly, the servant staggered and fell to the floor. He cried out in pain, and could not get up. "Help me!" he cried.

Maximilian and Valentine ran out to call for the doctor. Meanwhile, Villefort had come into the room. He stared in horror as the old servant clutched at his chest. When the doctor arrived, it was too late to help the poor man. He was dead within the hour.

Maximilian and Valentine had already left the

room when the doctor held the lemonade to his nose. "Poison!" he cried. "The same poison that killed the Marquise."

"Death is in my house!" moaned Villefort.

"No, monsieur," said the doctor. "*Murder* is in your house!" The doctor told Villefort that the poison must have been meant for Noirtier. "But the murderer didn't know that the lemonade could not harm the old man. No one knew that I've been treating him with small amounts of this poison for a rare illness. His body has gotten used to it."

The doctor suggested that Valentine must be the murderer. She was the one who had served the lemonade. "That's impossible!" Villefort cried angrily. "My daughter is not guilty." But the doctor insisted that Valentine would have the most to gain. She would, after all, inherit all of Noirtier's money—just as she had inherited from the Marquise.

"Please *think*, monsieur," said the doctor as he was leaving. "If you insist on protecting a murderer in your home, I will have nothing more to do with this family."

§10 Blinded by Greed

Caderousse was looking for Benedetto. The 200 francs he had been receiving each month were no longer enough for him. He needed more money in order to live well. He finally found Benedetto in his hotel room. "It's not enough—I need more money," Caderousse demanded rudely.

"I'm sorry. I cannot give you anymore," said Benedetto.

"You *say* you're sorry! But all you would have to do is ask the Count of Monte Cristo for more money," said Caderousse. "Wait a minute. I have an even better idea. Tell me where the count keeps his money and how I can get into his house."

Benedetto quickly told him what he needed to know. But as soon as Caderousse left, Benedetto wrote a note to the count. He warned that an enemy would break into the count's house that night. When Dantes read the note, he prepared to catch the thief. He waited for hours in the hall outside his bedroom. Finally, at about a quarter to 12, he heard a footstep on the balcony. Someone was climbing through the bedroom window!

In the dim light inside the bedroom, Dantes got a good look at the intruder. It was none other than Caderousse! Under the cover of darkness, Dantes went to his dressing room and changed into his priest's outfit. He then walked into the bedroom.

Caderousse had been trying to break into the desk. He looked up, startled. "You're the priest who gave me the diamond!" he cried. "What are you doing here?"

"You have a good memory," said Dantes. "Why are you trying to rob the Count of Monte Cristo?"

"I don't have enough money to live as I would like to," was all Caderousse could think to say.

"It seems that you *never* have enough money," said Dantes. "The diamond wasn't enough for you, either. And now this."

"*What?* You know about the diamond trader?" Caderousse gasped. "I beg you, take pity on me. I am a poor man. Poverty made me do it!" he whined.

"No, it was your greed that made you do it. But I'll take pity on you if you tell me the truth," said

Dantes. "Tell me everything—starting with how you learned the floor plan of this house."

Caderousse began by telling Dantes about Benedetto. "That young criminal has fooled everyone into thinking he is the rich young Andrea Cavalcanti," said Caderousse. "He gets money from the Count of Monte Cristo—and *I* get money from him. Soon he will marry Eugenie, the daughter of Baron Danglars. Then he will be truly rich."

"And you would allow him to get away with this?" said Dantes. "But I cannot permit it. I will write to Danglars—"

"That would be the end of my money," thought Caderousse. So before Dantes could finish his sentence, Caderousse pulled out a knife and thrust it at him. Luckily, Dantes was wearing a metal vest beneath his priest's robe. As the knife bounced off his chest, Dantes grabbed hold of Caderousse's arm and twisted it.

"Now you're going to write what *I* tell you," said Dantes. He put a pen in Caderousse's hand. Caderousse wrote a note to Danglars, telling all about Benedetto and what he'd been up to. When he had finished, Dantes took the note. "Now you can go," he growled. "If you get home safely, I'll

believe that God has forgiven you—and I will
forgive you also." Earlier, Dantes had seen someone
lurking outside in the dark. He knew that
Caderousse was in danger.

Caderousse went out the window and climbed
to the ground. Suddenly he cried out, "Help! I've
been stabbed!" Dantes ran downstairs. By the time
he reached Caderousse, the attacker had already
fled. Caderousse was lying on the ground. "It was
Benedetto!" he gasped. "Let me add something to
that note. I want to be sure that Danglars knows
who stabbed me."

While Caderousse wrote, Dantes said, "I'll call for a doctor."

"It's too late for that," Caderousse gasped. "Why didn't you stop Benedetto from stabbing me?"

"God gave you good health, work, and good friends—and you threw everything away," said Dantes. "God sent you a huge diamond, and you became a murderer. If you were truly sorry for what you had done, I would have helped you. But I simply allowed God's will to be done."

"I don't believe in God," said Caderousse.

"Ah, but there *is* a God," said Dantes. "And there is justice. Look me in the eyes. Don't you recognize me?"

Caderousse stared at Dantes, but it was too dark to see his face clearly. "Who are you?" he asked in a weak voice.

"One of your oldest friends, the one you betrayed. I am Edmond Dantes!" said Dantes.

Caderousse struggled to speak. "So there is a God, after all," he gasped. "Forgive me, Lord, forgive me. You are the father of men in heaven and the judge of men on earth!" Those were Caderousse's last words. Dantes waited beside his body until the doctor and Villefort arrived.

 **Web of Revenge**

One by one, Dantes' enemies got caught in the web of revenge he had been spinning. With Caderousse out of the way, Dantes next turned his attention to Fernand. In a few days, an article in the newspaper made a terrible accusation against Fernand de Morcerf. It said that he had betrayed the Greek leader, Ali Pasha. No one knew who had made that accusation. It was an anonymous writer who had sent a letter to the newspaper.

Fernand was then called to court to testify before a government committee. He told how he had bravely tried to defend Ali Pasha against the Turks. But then the committee called a witness—a beautiful young woman called Haydee. "I recognize you," she cried, angrily pointing her finger at Fernand. "You're the man who betrayed my beloved father, Ali Pasha. My father's blood is on your hands!"

The committee judged Fernand to be guilty. In a state of shock, Fernand fled from the court. When Albert heard the news, he grew angry. He learned that Danglars had written to Greece for information—at the request of the Count of Monte Cristo! "So Monte Cristo is behind this," Albert thought. "He'll pay for ruining my father's name!"

Albert sent word to Dantes, challenging him to a duel the following morning. When Mercedes learned of this, she went to see Dantes. "Edmond, I beg you, don't kill my son!" she cried.

Dantes told her that he had sworn revenge against Fernand. He had no wish to kill Albert. But since the young man had challenged him to a duel, he had no choice but to accept.

Mercedes insisted that *she* was the guilty one. It was she, after all, who did not wait for Dantes while he was in prison. Then Dantes showed her the letter that Danglars had written and Fernand had mailed. "I recently bought this," said Dantes. "*This* is the reason for my revenge!"

When Mercedes read the letter, she cried out pitifully, overcome with grief. She fell to her knees, begging Dante's forgiveness. "God brought me here to punish the wicked!" he insisted.

Mercedes pleaded, "Punish the guilty, Edmond. But my son has done nothing wrong—he is innocent! Must I see the man I loved become the murderer of my son?"

At these words, Dantes suddenly knew that he could not kill Albert. He promised Mercedes that her son would live. Mercedes thanked Dantes and kissed his hand. But Dantes thought, "By sparing Albert's life, I am giving up my own life."

The next morning, Dantes and Albert met in the woods where the duel was to take place. Albert said, "I have learned of the terrible things my father did to you. You were right to punish him. Please accept my apology." The two shook hands.

Soon after Dantes returned home, Fernand arrived. He was boiling with rage. He accused Dantes of telling lies about him and demanded that they fight a duel. "But first tell me who you really are. I know nothing about you."

Dantes went out of the room and returned shortly, dressed as a sailor. Fernand's eyes grew wide. *"Edmond Dantes!"* he cried out in horror. Then he ran from the room.

Upon returning home, Fernand saw Mercedes and Albert getting into a carriage. They did not see him. He heard Mercedes say, "This is no longer our home, and Morcerf is no longer our name. We will use my father's name, Herrera." At that, Fernand's world came crashing down around him. He ran upstairs and found his gun. He fired one shot—and fell to the floor, dead.

Meanwhile, Dantes was at Danglars' house. Guests had gathered there for the wedding announcement of Danglars' daughter Eugenie and Andrea Cavalcanti. Villefort had not yet arrived, and only Dantes knew why. He had just sent Villefort Caderousse's note about Cavalcanti.

Suddenly a policeman entered the salon and asked Danglars to point out Cavalcanti. "The man is an escaped prisoner, accused of murdering Caderousse," said the policeman. As soon as Benedetto saw the policeman, he moved closer to the door. While the others were talking, he slipped outside and ran away. The police found him later, however, and arrested him.

Dantes' plan for Danglars was proceeding smoothly. A few days later, Dantes took five million francs from his account at Danglars' bank. Danglars had boasted about his bank's huge fortune. But now the bank's cash reserves were running low.

Later that day, another customer asked for the same amount, and Danglars fell into a panic. He told the man to come back the next day. Meanwhile, Danglars made plans to flee the country. He would take with him whatever money was left in the bank.

Both Caderousse and Fernand were now dead—and Danglars' life was falling apart. At last the time had come for Dantes to destroy his last enemy, Villefort. He went to Villefort's house to visit Valentine. She was resting in bed. Maximilian explained that she had not been well lately. Dantes learned that old Noirtier had been giving her some of his own medicine for her protection. Now Dantes told Valentine, "Pretend to be asleep, and you will see who the murderer is."

That afternoon, Heloise went into Valentine's room. Valentine saw her pour something into the glass of water by the bed. The girl was shocked that her stepmother could be so evil. Later, she told Dantes what had happened. He gave her a small pill and told her she would no longer be in danger. "No matter what happens—even if you wake up in a coffin or a tomb—don't worry. Just remember that I will be watching over you."

Valentine swallowed the pill and fell into a deep

sleep. Everyone thought that she had died. Even the doctor said she was dead. Villefort and old Noirtier were crushed, as was Maximilian when he heard the news. Heloise pretended to be upset—until the doctor began to test the liquid in Valentine's glass. Then she fainted.

Dantes, now dressed as the priest, prepared Valentine's body for the funeral. The funeral procession was so painful for Maximilian that he thought about ending his life. Seeing this, Dantes stopped him and told him to have hope. "Within a month, my friend, we will all be very happy."

Meanwhile, Villefort was busy preparing for Benedetto's trial. It was then that Noirtier told him that the murders in his house were committed by his own wife, Heloise! Villefort was shaken by this news. But he assured the doctor that justice would soon be done.

Alone with Heloise, Villefort demanded, "Where do you keep your poison?"

"I don't know what you're talking about," Heloise answered in a shaky voice.

"I know what you've done," Villefort said coldly. "But I can't let you ruin the family name. Where is the rest of the poison?"

Heloise frantically begged her husband, "Have mercy on me! I'm your *wife!* Don't do this!"

Villefort said, "I repeat, justice must be done! I am going to the court now to demand the death penalty for a murderer! If I find you alive when I return, you will be in prison by tonight!" Villefort turned away from his wife and left the house.

In the courtroom, Benedetto was on trial. When the judge asked him about his name, he said, "I've had many names—but my father's name is Villefort!" He smiled and pointed to the prosecutor. "That man tried to bury me alive when I was an infant. I was saved by some kind people. Yet, even so, when I grew up, I lived a life of crime. Yes, I have been a thief and a murderer!"

All eyes in the court turned to Villefort, who slumped down in his chair. He was staring at the floor, thinking, "God's justice has caught up with me!" As he left the court, Villefort thought, "I hope Heloise has not yet taken my advice. What right did I have to judge her? We will leave France and start a new life with our son Edward." But when he returned home, a final horror awaited him. There on the bedroom floor was his wife Heloise, and next to her was Edward. Both were dead.

As Villefort staggered through the house in a daze, he came across Dantes, still dressed as a priest. Dantes took one look at Villefort and knew what must have happened in the courtroom. "I believe that you have now been punished enough for your evil deeds," he said.

Villefort stared at Dantes in disbelief. "I recognize that voice!" he said. "Why, you're the Count of Monte Cristo!"

"Look again!" Dantes said coldly. "Don't you remember the man you locked away so many years ago? Have you forgotten the boy you left to die a slow, terrible death in the Chateau d'If?"

"*Oh, my God!*" cried Villefort. "You're Edmond Dantes!" He grabbed Dantes' arm and led him to the bedroom. "Are you happy now?" he cried. "Is your revenge now complete?" Villefort then ran out into the garden, moaning and screaming. He called out wildly to his son Edward. It was clear to Dantes that Villefort's mind had snapped. The man had gone mad.

Dantes felt empty as he looked down at the bodies of Heloise and Edward. For the first time, he began to wonder if he had gone too far in carrying out his revenge.

12 The Power of Love

His work being done, it was time for Dantes to leave Paris. So he traveled to Marseilles, taking Maximilian with him. The young man could not stop grieving over the loss of Valentine. He had no wish to go on living. But Dantes often told him, "You must live and hope. Always remember that those we have lost to death live on forever in our hearts."

In Marseilles, Maximilian went to visit his friends, while Dantes went to see Mercedes. She had been weeping because her son Albert had joined the army. Now she was all alone. Telling her not to worry, Dantes assured her that Albert would make a good life for himself. Mercedes thanked Dantes for saving her son's life. "I was just carrying out God's plan," he said. The truth was, however, that he now had doubts about the disaster he had brought to his enemies.

After leaving Mercedes, Dantes visited the

Chateau d'If—which was no longer a prison. A guide took him to his old cell, and then to the cell of Father Faria. He showed Dantes the book that the old priest had written on cloth.

Dantes looked through the book. He saw the words, *Thou shalt tear out the teeth of the dragon and trample the lions underfoot, sayeth the Lord.* Dantes thought about the meaning of the old priests' words. "Maybe I was right after all," he thought. "The wicked must be punished, and my revenge was just!"

When Dantes returned to Marseilles, Maximilian was still in a gloomy mood. Dantes said, "I must go to Italy now. Promise to meet me on the Isle of Monte Cristo when I return." The sad young man promised to do so.

Dantes had unfinished business to attend to in Italy. When Danglars had fled with the bank's money, he had gone to Rome. There, according to a plan worked out by Dantes and Luigi Vampa, he had become the bandit's prisoner. Vampa offered food to his prisoner—but he demanded 100,000 francs per meal! The greedy Danglars had refused to pay. "Why, this is robbery! I simply won't eat," he declared in outrage.

But as the days went by, Danglars grew weaker and weaker. Finally, he gave in to his hunger and agreed to pay for his meals. Before long, Danglars' money was all gone. "Now what's going to happen to me?" he wondered. "Do they mean to kill me?"

One day Danglars heard a voice in the darkness. "Do you repent for the evil you have done?" the voice asked. Danglars turned around. In the shadows he saw a man wearing a cloak.

"Yes, I repent!" Danglars cried.

"Then I forgive you!" the man in the cloak said, as he stepped closer. "I forgive you—because I myself need to be forgiven."

"The Count of Monte Cristo!" cried Danglars.

"No, I am not a count," said Dantes. "I am the man you so cruelly betrayed many years ago. I am Edmond Dantes!"

Danglars fell to the floor in shock. When he came to, he was lying alongside a road. He crawled down to a stream to drink some water. When he looked at his reflection in the water, he saw that his hair had turned white!

Meanwhile, Dantes sailed from Italy to the Isle of Monte Cristo. When Maximilian arrived, he welcomed the young man and brought him to his grotto. Dantes could see that his young friend was unhappier than ever. Maximilian said sadly, "I'm afraid I've come to the end of my road."

"You can have anything you want, my friend," said Dantes. "Only live!"

"I cannot go on living without Valentine," said Maximilian.

After dinner, Dantes said, "You have suffered enough. This is what you asked for, and this is what I promised you." He gave Maximilian a liquid that made him go to sleep. Then he called Valentine into the room to see Maximilian.

Maximilian's eyes flickered. He thought he saw Valentine's face. "Is this heaven? Is this death?" he wondered. His lips moved, but there was no sound. Valentine rushed to his side.

"He's calling you in his sleep," said Dantes. "Death tried to keep you apart, but the power of love was too strong! You two must never leave each other again. I give you back to one another. May God give me credit for the two lives I have saved!"

Filled with joy, Valentine kissed Dantes' hand. "Do you love Haydee?" asked Dantes.

"With my whole heart," said Valentine.

"Well, then, I have a favor to ask of you," said

Dantes. "Protect her for me—because from now on, she will be alone in the world."

"Alone in the world?" said a voice from the doorway behind Dantes. "*Why?*"

Dantes turned around. Haydee was standing there, looking pale.

"Because, daughter of a prince, you must be free to take your place in the world," Dantes explained.

"Then you are leaving me?" Haydee asked sadly. The sorrow in Haydee's voice showed Dantes how deep her feelings were for him. "Don't send me away! I will die without you!" she gasped.

"Do you love me, then?" said Dantes.

"Oh, yes, I love you!" Haydee cried. "I love you as I love my life!" She ran into Dantes' arms.

"Let it be as you wish, my sweet angel!" Dantes cried. "I was going to punish myself for my acts of revenge. But it seems that God has forgiven me and wants me to be happy!" Dantes and Haydee said goodbye to Valentine and walked out of the grotto.

Within an hour, Maximilian woke up. "Oh, I still live!" he cried. Then he turned around and saw Valentine, who was at his side. With a loud cry, happy beyond words, Maximilian fell to his knees before her.

The next day, Maximilian and Valentine were walking arm in arm by the seashore. A sailor from Dantes' boat found them and handed Maximilian a note from Dantes. It said:

My dear Maximilian, a boat is waiting to take you to Noirtier. He wishes to give his granddaughter Valentine his blessing before you get married. My house in Paris is your wedding present.

Tell Valentine to pray for me. I once thought I was the equal of God in handing out rewards and punishments. I now know that true power and wisdom belong to God alone.

Maximilian, I've learned that only a man who has truly suffered can be truly happy. That is why I have let you suffer as you did.

Live and be happy, dear children of my heart. Never forget that all human wisdom is in these words: Wait and hope.

Your friend, Edmond Dantes

"Where is the count?" Maximilian asked the sailor. The man pointed to a tiny white sail on the far blue horizon. "Who knows if we shall ever see them again," said Maximilian.

"My dear," said Valentine, "remember what the count said. We can only wait and hope."